A GOLDEN BOOK • NEW YORK
Western Publishing Company, Inc., Racine, Wisconsin 53404

# THE BIG GOLDEN BOOK OF
# CAVEMEN
## AND OTHER PREHISTORIC PEOPLE

By Robert A. Bell
Illustrated by Gabriele Nenzione
and Mauro Cutrona

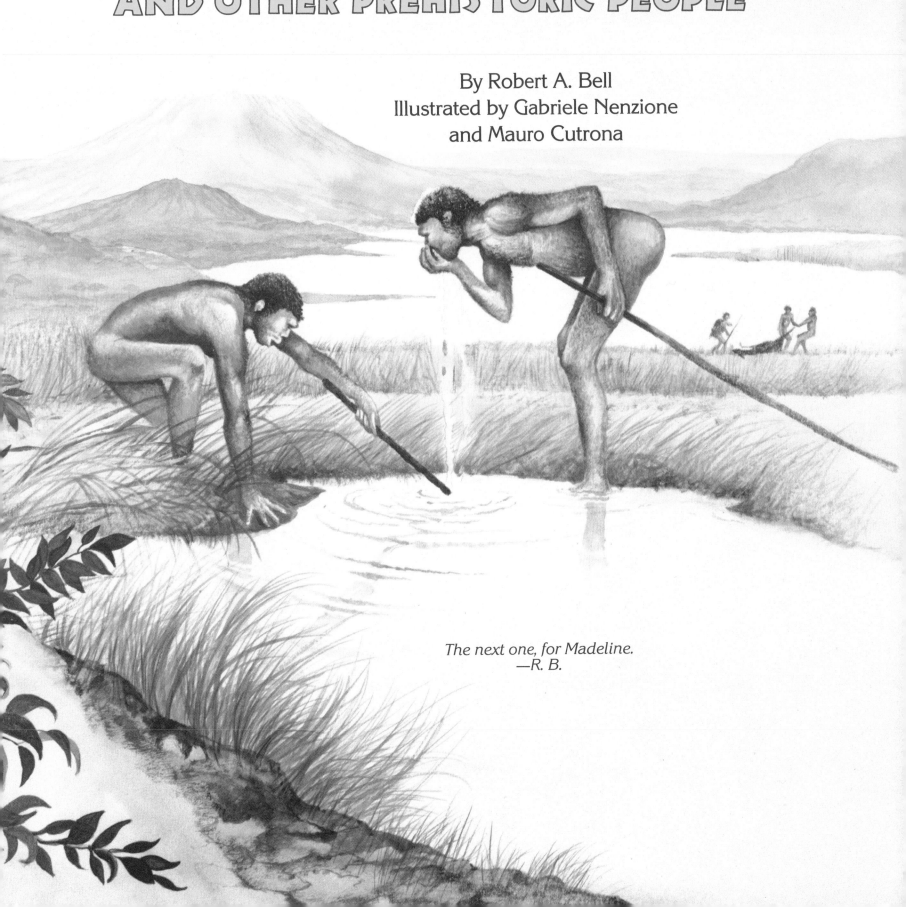

*The next one, for Madeline.*
*—R. B.*

# Table of Contents

Dinosaurs: Giant Earthshakers ................................................8

The Biggest Disaster ..........................................................10

Changing Mammals, Changing Earth .........................................12

A Very Special Creature: "Skillful Man" ......................................14

What Makes Us Human: Two Legs, Two Hands, and a Large Brain ........16

Fitting Into the World .........................................................19

The Power of Adaptation .....................................................20

Sharing ........................................................................22

The Hominids .................................................................24

Different Tastes ..............................................................26

How Can We Know So Much? ................................................28

Moving North .................................................................31

Standing Man ................................................................32

Skills of Survival .............................................................34

What Happened to *Homo habilis*? .........................................36

People of the Neander River .................................................38

Honoring the Dead ..........................................................40

The Coming of the Ice .......................................................43

Paintings Underground .......................................................44

Masters of the Horse? ........................................................46

Bridges Over the Sea .........................................................48

All Corners of the Globe .....................................................50

The Melting of the Ice .......................................................52

The First Farmers ............................................................54

A New Way of Life ...........................................................56

Wealth and Power ...........................................................58

Index ..........................................................................60

# Dinosaurs: Giant Earthshakers

One hundred fifty million years ago, several kinds of animals roamed the Earth. Frogs, toads, and other **amphibians** were among the first creatures on land. They were soon followed by lizards, snakes, and other small **reptiles.** These creatures, however, never grew as big as their later reptile cousins: the dinosaurs.

Dinosaurs, in fact, came in all sizes, from ones smaller than a chicken to giants like the Ultrasaurus (UL-trah-SORE-us), which measured 100 feet from nose to tail. Weighing about 200,000 pounds, Ultrasaurus must have made the earth shake when it walked. Dinosaurs lived everywhere—in swamps, forests, mountains and valleys, grasslands and deserts. Some even lived in the sea and others are thought to have flown through the air.

## Hidden Creatures

A fourth kind of animal was hard to find. There weren't many of them, and they were all quite small. They hid in holes in the ground and under rocks and fallen trees. They scurried from hiding place to hiding place in search of seeds and nuts and fruit and insects. And the ground *never* shook when they walked.

They were **mammals.** Unlike dinosaurs, other reptiles, and amphibians, they had hair on their bodies. Instead of laying eggs as the others did, they gave birth to live young, which they fed with milk from their bodies. Mammals were warm-blooded, which means that their bodies stayed the same temperature inside no matter how warm or cold it got outside. Reptiles and amphibians were cold-blooded, which means that their body temperature rose and fell with the weather. Scientists today disagree on whether dinosaurs were warm- or cold-blooded.

In addition to land animals, there were fish in the sea as well as insects crawling on the ground or flying through the air. But all the big animals were dinosaurs. In fact, for 130 million years, *every* large animal on Earth was a dinosaur. The rest of the world's creatures did their best to stay out of the groundshakers' way.

## The Biggest Disaster

Scientists are still arguing about *why* it happened. But everyone agrees on *what* happened. About 65 million years ago, in what must have been the greatest natural disaster of all time, the dinosaurs disappeared.

Perhaps a giant meteor or comet fell from space and struck the Earth like a terrible, fiery hammer. Such a shock would have caused mighty earthquakes. Huge tidal waves would have crossed the seas and ravaged the land. Volcanoes would have flashed into flame and darkened the sky with dust and smoke.

Or maybe it was something less sudden and terrible—but just as deadly. Whatever happened, in a fairly short time most of the world's large land animals, flying animals, and swimming animals died out.

## The Survivors

Some animals lived through the terrible changes. Many of the smaller creatures survived. There were still frogs, toads, crocodiles, and turtles; lizards, snakes, insects, and fish. There were birds, too, which had first appeared during the time of the dinosaurs. And there were still mammals.

Over the next 60 million years, many changes took place. Some of the survivors grew larger and filled the place in nature left by the dinosaurs. In almost every case, they were mammals. From the survivors of the disaster sprang the thousands of different mammals that live in the swamps, forests, mountains and valleys, grasslands and deserts today—including the ones now reading this book.

# Changing Mammals, Changing Earth

As they changed, mammals took on many strange and surprising shapes. The plant-eating *Moropus* (MOR-o-puss) looked like a cross between a horse and a lion. *Megatherium* (meg-a-THER-ee-um) looked like today's opossum, but it was big enough to knock over trees. One of the early mammals was the saber-toothed cat. Some lighthearted scientist named it *Smilodon* (SMILE-o-don).

The Earth continued to change, too, during this time. It was much warmer than it is today. It was so warm that there was little or no ice at the North and South Poles. This meant there was more water in the oceans. The bigger oceans covered more of the land, and so the continents were smaller than they are now.

*Moropus*

*Megatherium*

*Smilodon*

# The Continents Divide

The continents were also in different places. While the dinosaurs were alive, all the land on Earth was a single gigantic continent now called Pangea (pan-JEE-a). By the time the dinosaurs died out 65 million years ago, Pangea had begun to break up. The pieces moved slowly, each carrying mammals and other creatures. By 2 million years ago, they had nearly reached their present positions.

After 60 million years of change, most of the mammals had become animals you would recognize today. In Africa, there were zebras and monkeys and apes, lions and hyenas and rhinoceroses. There were still surprises, of course, like the giant hairy elephant known as the woolly mammoth. But it was a world that did not look unlike Africa today—except for one very special creature.

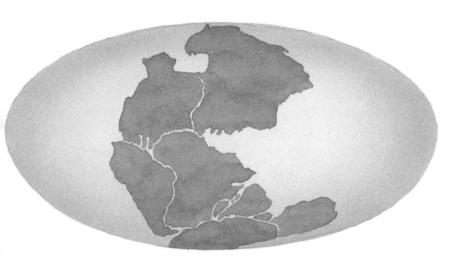

Pangea, over 100 million years ago

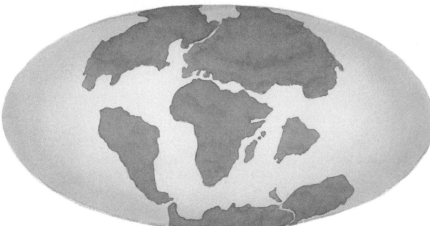

50 million years ago

2 million years ago

## A Very Special Creature: "Skillful Man"

We think that this creature lived in Africa about 2 million years ago, because its bones have been found there. And after careful study, scientists have named it *Homo habilis* (Ho-mo HA-bill-iss), the Latin words for "man" and "skillful."

What was special about *Homo habilis*? We believe that they were the first humanlike creatures—or **hominids**—on Earth. As hairy and strange as they looked, they were the ancestors of every person alive today.

How did they live? What did they eat? How did they act? The more scientists study these first people, the better they are able to answer one of the world's biggest questions: How did our ancestor *Homo habilis* turn into us?

14

# How *Homo habilis* Lived

We believe that *Homo habilis* lived in small groups. There were probably six or seven families in each group. They did not build houses or make clothes, because they didn't know how. They lived, worked, and rested in the hot sun and cooling rain. They probably spent as many hours searching for food as you spend in school. The rest of the time they played or rested or explored.

Because their survival depended on hunting and gathering food, *Homo habilis* did not live in just one place. Instead, groups moved camp as often as every few weeks. They moved because they had eaten up much of the food in one place, or because a nearby river had dried up and they needed water.

*Homo habilis* ate both plant foods and meat. Mostly, they ate plants—leaves, seeds, roots, nuts, and fruit—because these were easiest to find. Meat was harder to come by, since it could run away on four legs or fly. So most of the meat came from animals that had died from old age or sickness, or from what was left after a lion had finished its meal. And they didn't cook their meat, because they didn't know how to use fire.

# What Makes Us Human:
# Two Legs, Two Hands, and a Large Brain

*Homo habilis* were much more human than they looked—which is another way of saying that they were very different from the animals around them. For one thing, they walked standing up on two legs. Most animals—from cats and dogs to mice and elephants—walk on four legs. Even apes and monkeys, which sometimes walk on two legs, usually move around with their hands on the ground.

The hands themselves were different, too. Try touching the tip of your thumb to the tips of all your other fingers on the same hand. For a human being, it's easy. Some apes can do it, too, but not half as well as you can. The way our fingers and thumb are arranged lets us pick up things like pencils and screwdrivers and effectively use them as tools. Because *Homo habilis* had this distinctly human hand, scientists called them "skillful."

The final thing that made *Homo habilis* different was the size of the brain and how it was organized. Only half as big as a grown person's brain today, it was nearly twice the size of a chimpanzee's, and chimps are among the smartest animals. Pound for pound, *Homo habilis* had more brainpower than any other creature.

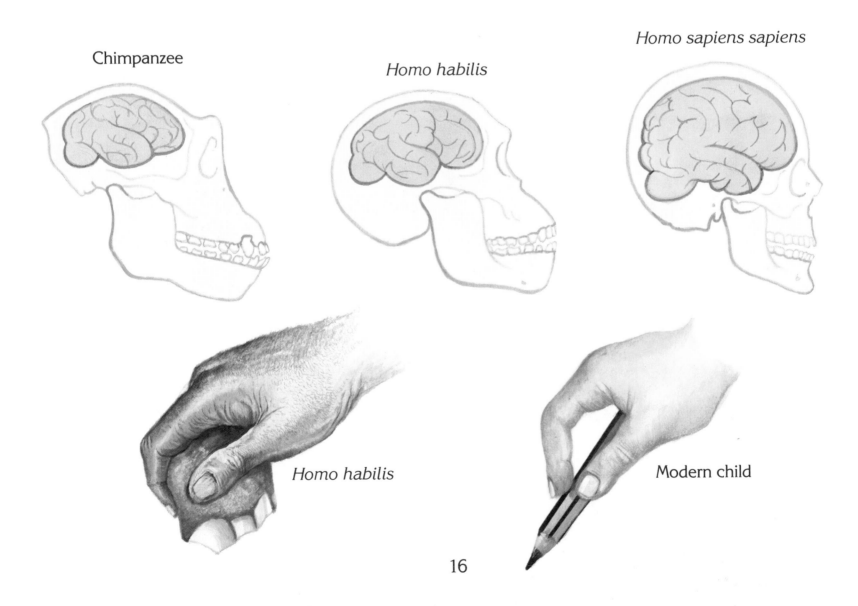

Chimpanzee

*Homo habilis*

*Homo sapiens sapiens*

*Homo habilis*

Modern child

# Fitting Into the World

Two-legged walking, thumbs, and big brains were very important for *Homo habilis*—and not just because you have them as well. It's really the other way around. You have these things today because they helped *Homo habilis* to adapt: to fit themselves to the world in new and better ways.

You began fitting yourself to the world as soon as you were born. You learned to walk, to talk, and to eat with a spoon. You learned to read and write and use numbers, and how to get along with others. And as you grow up, you will learn many other things needed in order to get a job and raise a family.

All creatures must fit themselves to the world they live in. They need to know where to find food and how to raise their children safely. And they need to know how to escape from other creatures who would like to eat them for dinner.

## Where They Belong

Animals are born knowing much of what they need to know. This is called *instinct*—nobody has to teach a fish to swim. By the time they grow up, they fit perfectly into their worlds. That's important. When you see animals in their natural environments, such as the snow and ice or the burning-hot desert, you may think how uncomfortable they must be. But wild penguins love the freezing water and snowy sky. Desert camels need a hot, dry place. If you tried to make them live elsewhere, they might die. It would be too hot or too cold; they couldn't find the food they need; and they wouldn't know how to protect themselves from danger. They *adapt,* or fit themselves, to their world, and that's where they belong.

19

## The Power of Adaptation

Adaptation—fitting yourself into the world—is a very slow but powerful process. It explains how, after millions of years, the descendants of *Homo habilis* could stop searching the forest for food and drive a car to the supermarket instead.

Walking on two feet let *Homo habilis* do something amazing: They could *carry* things in their hands. That may not sound very amazing—but just try to get through a single day *without* carrying something in your hands. Unless you stay in bed all day, it can't be done.

One of the most important things that *Homo habilis* could carry was food. Other animals eat their food where they find it—and are often chased from it by other animals who find it easier to steal a meal than find their own. By carrying food to a safe place, *Homo habilis* were able to keep more food to eat.

## Toolmaker

*Homo habilis*'s hands were also perfect for the most efficient use of tools: a stick, a sharp piece of stone, a big rock. These tools let *Homo habilis* dig in the ground for roots to eat. They could cut through the skin of dead animals to get at the meat. They could break bones to find the tasty marrow inside.

Almost all other animals use "tools" that are parts of their bodies. Lions use their claws and teeth for tearing. The long neck of a giraffe lets it reach leaves at the tops of trees. *Homo habilis* had none of these things—but they could make and use tools, and that let them eat just about anything they wanted.

## Brainpower at Work

In the daily struggle for food and safety, *Homo habilis*'s best tool was a large, complex brain. It gave them ideas: how to carry food to safety, to make tools, and to work together. Without such ideas, their other tools weren't worth much.

Imagine that three *Homo habilis* hunters find the half-eaten body of a zebra. They begin to drag it toward camp. But, smelling the food, twenty wild dogs come running. Crazed with hunger, they face the two-legged creatures. It looks as if the *Homo habilis* must choose between food or their lives.

But then one *Homo habilis* picks up a heavy stick. The others do the same. The dogs close in, moving a few steps forward and then a step back, growling, then coming ever closer. The leader of the pack leaps forward, jaws open wide. A *Homo habilis* jumps back, screaming. He swings his stick—and the wild dog goes down, stunned. Another dog charges and falls beneath the stick, and the rest of the dogs back away. Two *Homo habilis* begin to drag the zebra again, while the third follows, stick in hand, keeping a wary eye on the dogs.

# Sharing

Believe it or not, what made the most difference to *Homo habilis* (and set them most apart from other animals) was not their bodies. It was how they *acted*.

*Homo habilis* shared things—work and food—and they cooperated when danger threatened. If this does not seem surprising, it's because our lives today are based on sharing. We share food with our families and friends. We share schools and playgrounds, and factories and office buildings. We share so much that when somebody *doesn't* share, we get mad and yell, "That's not fair!"

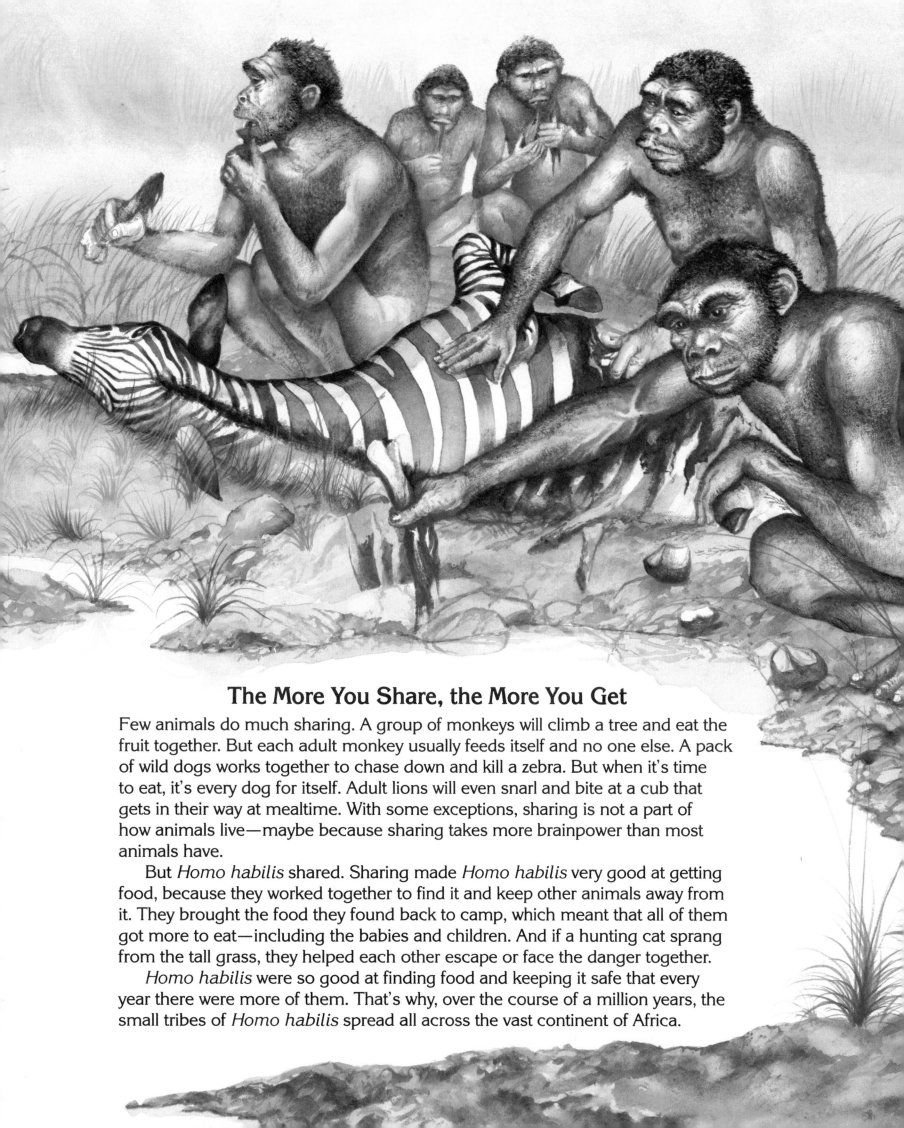

## The More You Share, the More You Get

Few animals do much sharing. A group of monkeys will climb a tree and eat the fruit together. But each adult monkey usually feeds itself and no one else. A pack of wild dogs works together to chase down and kill a zebra. But when it's time to eat, it's every dog for itself. Adult lions will even snarl and bite at a cub that gets in their way at mealtime. With some exceptions, sharing is not a part of how animals live—maybe because sharing takes more brainpower than most animals have.

But *Homo habilis* shared. Sharing made *Homo habilis* very good at getting food, because they worked together to find it and keep other animals away from it. They brought the food they found back to camp, which meant that all of them got more to eat—including the babies and children. And if a hunting cat sprang from the tall grass, they helped each other escape or face the danger together.

*Homo habilis* were so good at finding food and keeping it safe that every year there were more of them. That's why, over the course of a million years, the small tribes of *Homo habilis* spread all across the vast continent of Africa.

# The Hominids

*Homo habilis* may have appeared 3 to 5 million years ago. By 2 million years ago, they may have lived throughout Africa. But they were not the only hominids. In fact, for a long time, scientists found no trace of any hominid they were willing to call *homo,* meaning an ancestor of human beings today. Instead, they found many bones of hominids that they called **australopithecines** (AW-stru-lo-PITH-eh-seens).

There were at least two kinds of australopithecines, *Australopithecus africanus* (AW-stru-lo-PITH-eh-kuss aff-rih-CAN-us) and *Australopithecus robustus* (AW-stru-lo-PITH-eh-kuss roh-BUS-tuss). *A. robustus* was bigger, but both were bigger and heavier than *Homo habilis.* They also walked on two legs and had humanlike hands, but both had much smaller brains than *Homo habilis.*

*Australopithecus africanus*

*Australophitecus robustus*

24

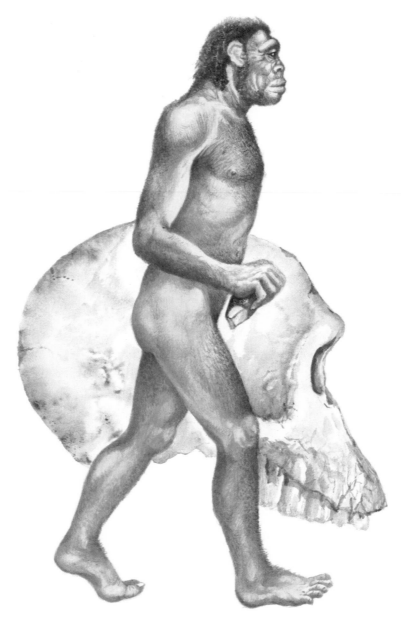

*Homo habilis*

## Ancestors or Cousins?

For many years, scientists thought that the australopithecines lived long before *Homo habilis* and were their ancestors, just as *Homo habilis* is our ancestor. But recently scientists have learned a curious thing: The australopithecines and *Homo habilis* lived side by side, sharing the same African homeland for millions of years. The australopithecines were actually cousins of *Homo habilis*.

This fact is curious because creatures that are much alike hardly ever share a homeland for long. If they eat the same foods and live in the same ways, they *compete* too much with each other. Who will get the most from the land? In the contest for survival, the loser eventually dies.

5 million years ago

*Australopithecus africanus*

## Different Tastes

Since the australopithecines and *Homo habilis* did share a homeland, they must have been different in some key way. Many scientists believe that the australopithecines may have eaten mostly grasses, roots, and fruit, while *Homo habilis* ate a greater mix, including a fair amount of meat. By eating differently, the two hominids could have lived near each other without fighting over every meal.

Their different tastes in foods may explain another curious fact. After living throughout Africa for a couple of million years, the australopithecines became extinct, or died out. We will never know exactly why, but scientists have made many guesses. Maybe they did not share food as their cousins, *Homo habilis,* did. Perhaps they did not make and use tools. From studying bones, scientists have also noticed an important fact.

About the time that the australopithecines began to die out, there began to be many more baboons. Baboons are monkeys that live mostly on grasses, roots, and fruit, as we think the australopithecines did. Sharing a homeland with *two* kinds of similar creatures may have been too much. In the contest for food, the australopithecines could not compete with both the toolmaking *Homo habilis* and the baboons. And so they became extinct, leaving only one kind of hominid on the face of the Earth: our earliest ancestor, *Homo habilis.*

2 million years ago

*Australopithecus robustus*

*Homo habilis*

# How Can We Know So Much?

How do we know so much about creatures who lived so long ago? Their bones and tools tell a lot—though they are *very* hard to find. Scientists who study early man have a joke: There are more people studying than there are things to study.

Scientists often search for years without finding anything. Then it may rain hard one day and turn a small, trickling stream into a rushing river, which washes away dirt and rock along its banks. The next time scientists visit the area, they may see a tiny piece of bone sticking out of the ground.

That's when the hard work begins. Hour after hour, they dig and brush away the dirt that hides the bones or stone tools. Sometimes the bones must be painted with clear plastic on the spot to keep them from crumbling into dust.

When the bones and tools finally come out of the ground, scientists study them carefully. They compare them to the bones of animals and people today, looking for differences and similarities. Slowly, ideas develop about what early people looked like, what they ate, and how they lived.

## Testing Their Ideas

How do scientists make sense out of the information they gather? Some clues come from primitive tribes living today, like the bushmen of Africa, who live in the Kalahari Desert, and whose way of life has changed little for thousands of years. By watching them, scientists understand better the ancient bones and tools they have found.

They also check their ideas by experiment. One scientist made stone knives by breaking rocks into sharp-edged flakes. The stone flakes looked almost exactly like *Homo habilis* tools. Using these stone knives to cut up a dead animal was hard work, but the knives even cut through an animal hide an inch thick.

Europe

France

Asia

Africa

South
China
Sea

# Moving North

Two million years ago, all of the hominids in the world lived on the hot, dry plains of Africa. One million years later, they could be found from the coast of France to the South China Sea, throughout what is known as the Old World.

It was a big change. To see how big it was, you need to think about weather. In the parts of Africa where the hominids lived, there is a rainy season and a dry season. Days are usually hot. There is no snow, no ice, no winter at all. Plants grow fruit and nuts all year round. Animals live in the open year-round instead of sleeping through the winter as bears do, or going to warmer places as birds do.

But in Europe and much of Asia, the weather is completely different. During the winter, it is cold and snowy, and the trees go without leaves. There is little or nothing to eat for months at a time. Then, with the slow birth of spring, green shoots rise from the soil, and the trees swell with leaves. Flowers bloom and, as spring turns into summer, the land fills with fruit, nuts, and other food. But in all too short a time, summer's riches are buried again beneath snow and ice.

# Living Through Winter

How did *Homo habilis* survive this new, terrible thing: winter? For eons, they lived with food as close as the nearest fruit tree. How did they live in places where icy winds froze them and the food supply vanished for months?

They didn't. By the time human beings reached Europe and Asia, *Homo habilis* had disappeared. A new creature had taken their place.

# Standing Man

The creatures who moved into Europe and Asia were different from *Homo habilis*. For one thing, their bodies were almost exactly like ours today. If one of them showed up on Halloween wearing a mask, you might think he was a neighbor. But you'd change your mind fast when the mask came off.

Because their bodies were like those of modern man, scientists named them *Homo erectus*, "standing man." But how they looked was only part of the story.

## Changing the World to Suit Themselves

In *Homo erectus,* the large brain of *Homo habilis* had become even larger, though it was still not as big as in modern man. With more brainpower, *Homo erectus* made bigger and better stone tools, which let them do more work more easily. They also began to hunt, in addition to getting their meat from animals that were already dead. And they found new, clever ways to do it.

Places have been found where *Homo erectus* drove herds of animals into swamps to trap them in the mud. The trapped animals were easily killed by hunters. In one such place, scientists have found the bones of at least thirty elephants, six rhinoceroses, twenty-five deer, twenty-five horses, and ten oxen.

We think that *Homo erectus* also knew how to make bags and containers, which let them carry much more than their hands could hold. This invention let them gather food more easily and from farther away.

And, though we can't know exactly what kind of language they used, we know that *Homo erectus* communicated with each other. Perhaps they had only a few dozen words, but these enabled them to work together for the good of all.

## Skills for Survival

These skills and inventions kept *Homo erectus* alive through the winter. They went on eating mostly plant foods in the spring, summer, and fall. But when winter came, meat became their most important food. They *had* to be good enough hunters to bring meat home often.

Food was one thing. Keeping warm was another. *Homo erectus* were probably the first people to wear clothing, which they made from the skins of animals and tied around themselves with vines. They had also mastered fire.

How did they discover fire? It had always been part of their world. When thunderstorms crossed the land, lightning would start fires in the forests. One day a *Homo erectus* may have decided not to run away. Afraid but curious, he lifted a burning branch and began to see what this bright, hot thing could do.

It was a huge discovery, for fire soon warmed them and cooked their food. It also kept them safe at night, because fire frightens most animals. In other words, *Homo erectus* could now ignore all but the harshest weather and live just about wherever they wanted to live. And they seemed to want to live all over.

# The Accidental Travelers

*Homo erectus* didn't wake up one morning and say, "Hey, everybody, let's go to China!" Instead, it happened very slowly. Maybe some hunters walked farther than usual one day and saw an especially good place to camp. So the next time their group moved, they went over the next hill to this wonderful camping place. Maybe there was an even better place farther on.

And when their children grew up, they may have moved still farther. Every year there were more and more *Homo erectus*, and they all needed places to live where they could find food and water. And so, by chance, they became travelers.

# What Happened to *Homo habilis*?

*Homo erectus* was the name given to this new creature that spread all over the world. But what happened to good old "skillful man"—*Homo habilis*?

*Homo habilis* turned into *Homo erectus*—not all at once, and not by magic. The three special skills of *Homo habilis*—walking on two legs, using their hands, and having a large brain—were what made it happen.

## Why Homo erectus Won Out

Remember how all creatures try to get enough to eat, to raise their children safely, and to escape from other creatures who want to eat them? When a creature does these things well, there will soon be lots of its children and grandchildren all over the place, because they do these things well, too.

*Homo habilis* did these things very well. But some *Homo habilis* did them better than others. Some could run faster. Some were better at using their hands. And some were smarter—probably the most important thing of all.

The smarter they were, the better they would be at staying alive and raising children. Soon there would be families and then whole bands who were better at staying alive. The more that *Homo habilis* changed in the direction of *Homo erectus,* the more children they had who grew up to have children of their own.

The ones who did not change—who remained pure *Homo habilis*—were not as good at staying alive. Every year there were fewer and fewer of them, until, after thousands of years, they were gone. *Homo erectus,* who were smart enough to make better tools, to hunt big animals, and to use fire, survived.

37

# People of the Neander River

When bones or stone tools are dug up, how can we tell how old they are? There are no machines that can measure the age of *very* old things.

The only clue usually comes from the rocks nearby. Scientists can tell, after careful study, about how old the rock is. Knowing this, they also know about when the bones or tools first lay upon the ground and were covered by soil—layer after layer carried by wind and water. Over millions of years, the great weight of these layers squeezed the soil around the bones and tools into rock.

Using these clues, scientists have decided that *Homo habilis* and the australopithecines first appeared somewhere between 5 million and 3 million years ago. *Homo erectus* made their appearance about 1.5 million years ago, and for nearly 1.5 million years they slowly spread throughout the Old World. But then, about 100,000 years ago, a new creature appeared.

# The Neanderthals

The change was gradual. Many bones have been found that are mostly like those of *Homo erectus* but have one or two new features. These new features slowly took the place of the old, so scientists decided to give the new creature a new name. It's a mouthful: *Homo sapiens neanderthalensis* (HO-mo SAY-pee-ans nee-AN-der-thall-EN-sis). For short, we call them Neanderthals (nee-AN-der-thalls).

Part of their name comes from the Neander River in Germany. In a cave beside this river, the first Neanderthal bones were found. Another part of their name should be familiar by now: *homo,* meaning "man." But the middle word of their Latin name—*sapiens* or "intelligent"—is important. Modern human beings also have *sapiens* in their Latin name. The Neanderthals were the first modern human beings. Their full Latin name means "intelligent people of the Neander."

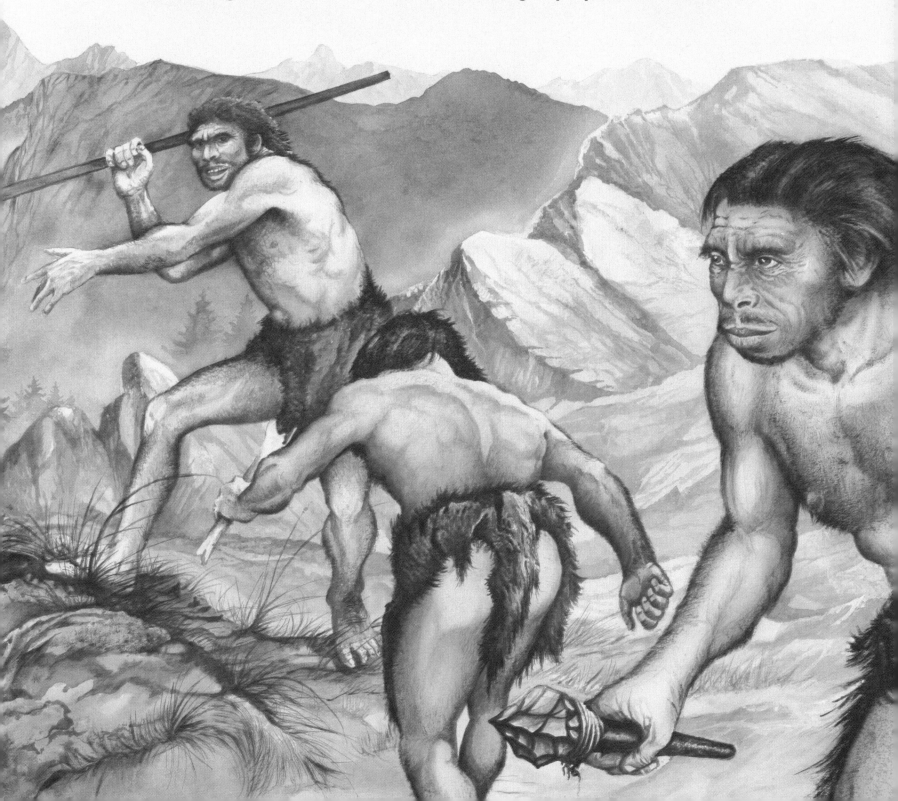

# Honoring the Dead

Neanderthals were as different from *Homo erectus* as *Homo erectus* was from *Homo habilis*. As always, the changes were in their bodies and in how they lived.

They were much more modern-looking than *Homo erectus*. In fact, they looked much like people today, although their foreheads were a little flatter, the brow a little heavier, and the nose and mouth stuck out a bit farther. Their bodies were larger and heavier than *Homo erectus,* and they were probably stronger than the average person today. Their brains were also much bigger than those of *Homo erectus.* Actually, they were bigger than *our* brains! But being organized differently, their brains would not have given the Neanderthals our brainpower.

## Flowers and Bones

The Neanderthals were also a step ahead of *Homo erectus* in skills. They invented many new kinds of stone tools, including spear points and cutters, and they began to make tools from bone as well. They built fireplaces of piled stones that made their fires burn better and last longer.

There are also signs that they lived in complex ways which remind us of our lives today. In the Shanidar (SHAN-ih-darr) cave in the mountains of Iraq, scientists have found a full skeleton of a man lying on his side in a shallow hole in the ground. Around him are the long-dead remains of flowers. The meaning is clear: The man was buried, as we bury our dead today, in a grave scattered with flowers. Many such Neanderthal graves have been found. Food was buried in some, while others contained animals bones, tools or other ritual signs.

Many Neanderthals are buried in the Shanidar cave. Some of them show signs of having been badly hurt. It was clear to scientists that they lived for a long time after they were hurt, which means that the Neanderthals must have cared for them.

These are the first clues as to how our early ancestors *felt*. We can imagine their sadness as they laid a friend in his grave. And we know that caring for the hurt, the sick, and the old takes patience, tenderness, and love. In the graves of Shanidar, we see the earliest signs of human beings at their best.

# The Coming of the Ice

About 100,000 years ago, the Neanderthals slowly began taking the place of *Homo erectus,* just as *Homo erectus* had replaced *Homo habilis* a million years earlier. Over the next 30,000 years, Neanderthals spread all over the world.

That's when the weather began to change. It would have been hard to tell at first. Winters were a little colder and snow stayed on the ground a bit longer.

But as the years passed, it grew still colder. The summers shrank and cooled. The winters became a freezing white eternity. The very oceans froze, forming great masses of ice at the North and South Poles, much of which is still there today.

In the far north country and on mountaintops, snow did not melt. With each passing year, it became deeper, icier, heavier. Finally, the great masses of ice and snow grew so heavy that they *moved.* They moved like slow white rivers, a mile high in some places, across the land. Called *glaciers* (GLAY-shurs), these great ice sheets carved the land, rubbed mountaintops smooth, dug lakes and river valleys. And they gave their name to the next 55,000 years. We call it the Ice Age.

The Ice Age changed the world. Many kinds of creatures that could not adapt to the cold died out. Others prospered and spread to new places. The Neanderthals were among them. Caves had always been handy homes; now they became the best of all places to live. A roof and walls of rock kept out the freezing weather, while fire warmed them. They grew much more skilled at making warm clothes. And hunting became more important than ever as the winters lengthened and the summers, when food grew, became ever shorter.

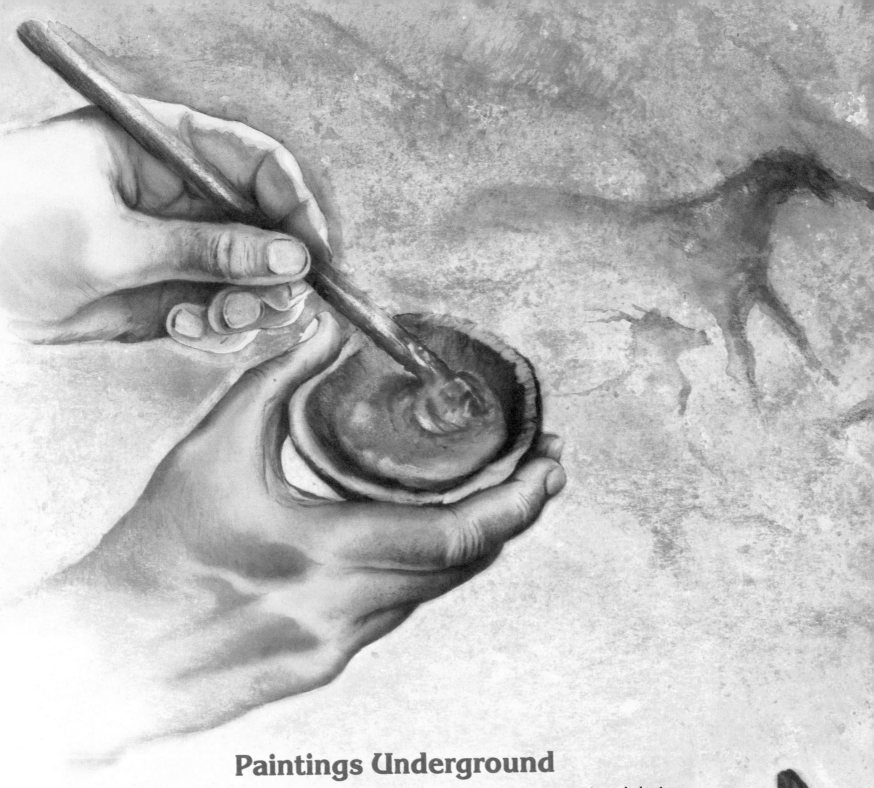

## Paintings Underground

Today you can visit caves in Spain and France and see pictures painted during the Ice Age. The paintings on the glistening rock walls are the work of skilled hands. They show horses and deer, lions and bulls in color. For the most part, one or two different colors were used—black and red were common. Occasionally, a third color appeared. There are even rare pictures of people. Some of the pictures are on walls deep within the caves. The artists must have crawled back into the fearful darkness, lighting their way with a flickering torch, to make a painting where few eyes would see it. What made them do it? Maybe the pictures were part of an early religion: the worship of the spirits of the animals they hunted.

Like many questions about early man, we cannot know for sure. But we do know that the makers of these magnificent paintings were not Neanderthals.

## The Arrival of Modern Man

The Ice Age gripped the world from 70,000 years ago until about 15,000 years ago. It was during this time, about 40,000 years ago, that modern people—people exactly like us—appeared. Scientists have given them the name *Homo sapiens sapiens* (HO-mo SAY-pee-ans SAY-pee-ans) to tell them apart from *Homo sapiens neanderthalensis.* And within a fairly short time, the Neanderthals disappeared, as had the people who came before them.

It was these new human beings—the smartest creatures ever to walk the Earth—who made the marvelous cave paintings of the Ice Age. They were the first artists in history to see a thing, remember it, and create it again with colored paints on a wall of rock. Of course, this is something every child can do today. But these were among the first pieces of art ever made. And, after thousands of years, the pictures are still powerful.

Cave painting was only one of countless ways in which *Homo sapiens* made their mark on the world.

## Masters of the Horse?

On the wall of a cave in La Marche (la MARSH), France, is a 14,000-year-old picture that has caused a lot of arguments. Some scientists think it offers an important clue about the way the new human beings lived. Others disagree.

The picture shows the head of a horse. The head has lines carved into it that look like a bridle—a set of ropes around a horse's head to give a rider something to hang on to. If those lines *are* a bridle, it means that people tamed horses long ago.

Scientists have been arguing about pictures like the one at La Marche for many years. The question regarding bridles is important because of what it may tell us about how *Homo sapiens sapiens* lived.

As hunters, human beings had only one use for horses—to eat when they got hungry. And they needed luck and skill just to get a meal, because wild horses, reindeer, and other wild animals don't just stand around waiting to be killed.

46

# New Uses for Animals

When people learned to tame animals, it made a huge change in their lives. They could go much farther and faster riding a horse. They could hunt a much bigger area and explore faraway places. With the animals' help, they could also carry much, much more from place to place.

Tame animals can provide food as well. Some of them, such as cows and goats, give milk. This was a completely new food for human beings, from which they would one day make cheese, yogurt, and butter. And tame animals were a handy way of storing meat—"on the hoof," as we say today.

Were people already taming animals 14,000 years ago? Or did this discovery come much later? There is some evidence of tame dogs as early as 12,000 years ago in Iraq! Questions like this are what make science exciting. Scientists will keep right on arguing until somebody finds a clue that proves the truth once and for all.

# Bridges Over the Sea

For nearly 1.5 million years, hominids had been living throughout Africa and the southern half of Europe and Asia. But neither *Homo erectus* nor the Neanderthals had moved into the far north. The winters there were too fierce, especially during the Ice Age.

But winter did not stop the new human beings. They went north to follow food: the huge herds of reindeer and bison that had adapted to the cold. *Homo sapiens sapiens* did not need to change physically to adapt to cold weather like the animals. They were smart, and they soon learned ways to survive and protect themselves in the most terrible cold. Slowly moving their camps as the herds moved, they traveled far to the north in Europe. Others traveled in Asia and even farther east. And there, they did something that would not be done again for many years: They discovered America.

## Across the Bering Strait

The Ice Age froze so much water into ice at the North Pole and the South Pole that the seas shrank. Much of what is now ocean bottom became dry land. About 40,000 years ago—and again about 18,000 years ago—the Bering Strait between Russia and Alaska was frozen grassland where glaciers wandered.

The herds of reindeer and bison crossed them and so did human beings. And as they had done everywhere else, the new human beings made this New World—as we still call it today—their home. With each passing century, they spread farther. By the time Columbus reached the New World, human beings were living from Alaska in the north to the southernmost tip of South America.

Asia

China

Pacific Ocean

Australia

New Zealand

# All Corners of the Globe

Human beings did not only go north. They spread to every corner of the globe. But to get there, they had to invent a completely new way to travel.

To the south and east of China (which is in Asia), the Pacific Ocean is filled with many thousands of islands. Most are small. Some are quite large, like New Zealand. One of them—Australia—is nearly as big as the United States.

# Sea Voyagers

When the seas shrank during the Ice Age, these islands all grew bigger than they are today. A few stopped being islands and joined the mainland. But the rest were still surrounded by the sea. Nevertheless, *Homo sapiens sapiens* found a way to reach them and make a home.

We don't know exactly how they did it. Perhaps they built rafts by tying logs together with rope. They may have made boats from reeds, as people still do in some parts of the world. But why did they make the journey? Were these early human beings already finding ways to get food from the sea? If so, they may have been searching for fish. Or possibly a great storm arose and swept them far out to sea where, by great luck, they found new lands. Maybe the desire to explore the unknown was as irresistible then as it is today. All we know for sure is that they did cross the seas, for their descendants live on these islands today.

Raft

Wooden Dugout

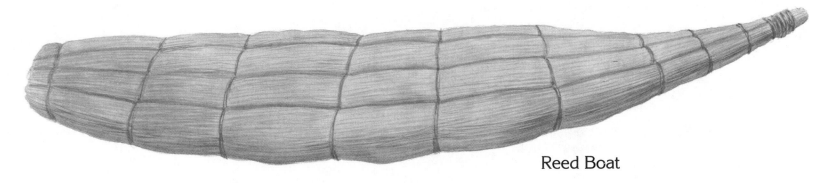

Reed Boat

# The Melting of the Ice

About 15,000 years ago, the Earth began to grow warm again. It took as long as the first coming of the ice. As centuries passed, the summers grew longer and warmer. The winters became less terrible. And the edges of the great glaciers began to melt. Slowly, over thousands of years, the new warmth melted the ice sheets, which retreated northward. Finally, by about 10,000 years ago, the weather was much as it is today.

With the warmer, wetter weather, the herds of reindeer and bison that had crossed Europe and Asia grew smaller. They stayed far in the cold north. Forests grew to cover the land. Rich grasslands spread. The seas rose. Islands grew more distant from each other and from the mainland.

## The Great Change

When bison and reindeer moved north and grassland turned to forest, people began to look for new kinds of food. As their ancestors had done before the Ice Age, they began to eat more plant foods as the warm summers grew longer.

Cave painting came to an end, as well, partly because people spent far less time in caves. They did not stop making art, but they turned to "portable art"— small sculptures and objects that could be taken from place to place.

Thus the stage was set for one of the greatest changes in history. This one did not happen *to* human beings. Instead, it was something that these beings *did.* Yet it would change the face of the Earth itself in only a few thousand years.

## The First Farmers

By the end of the Ice Age, scientists think, there were between 5 and 10 million people on Earth. Within 8,000 years, there were about *300 million* people. What made so huge an increase possible in so short a time?

In that part of the world we call the Middle East, two rivers run side by side for hundreds of miles. As the Ice Age ended, the land between the Tigris (TIE-griss) and the Euphrates (you-FRAY-tees) rivers became rich with grasses and plants. Among the grasses grew the wild ancestors of wheat, barley, beans, peas, and lentils. The people gathered these plants and found their seeds good to eat.

# Scattering Seeds

These people soon learned a tremendous amount about the ways of plants and animals. They probably understood that seeds were not just for eating—that seeds would also grow into plants. And one day someone must have held the seeds and wondered about them. It was summertime and there was plenty to eat. A few seeds would not be missed. So this person decided not to eat them—but to see what would happen if they were scattered where no plants grew.

It was such a simple thing. Other people may have tried it. They may have begun by clearing the weeds around plants to help them grow better. It probably took a long time for the idea to catch on—to plant seeds, to help them grow, and then to gather the harvest. But when it did catch on, it changed the way people lived forever. Instead of remaining hunters and gatherers moving from place to place, they became farmers who made permanent homes beside their fields.

## A New Way of Life

People began farming between the Tigris and Euphrates about 10,000 years ago. But it was not the only such place. About 7,000 years ago people in China also invented farming. In South America, they grew food about 5,000 years ago.

Why did people all over the world turn to farming?

This new question had the same answer: *food.* People could get far more food by farming than by gathering whatever happened to grow. And the plants they grew—wheat, barley, beans, peas, and lentils—could be dried and kept. For the first time since leaving Africa, people had plant foods to eat even in winter.

For millions of years hominids had changed by doing things that brought them more food. They weren't about to stop now.

## Villages and Towns

More food was just the beginning. When they had lived by hunting and gathering, people had to keep moving from place to place. But farmers *have* to stay in one place to take care of their crops. And the crops provide enough food for them to do it. So people began to build houses that were meant to last. They built them close to each other and to their fields. The first villages and towns were born.

With more food, people could feed still larger families. The extra people helped with the hard work of farming. And because they lived in one place, they began to make and keep *things*: tables and chairs, cooking pots and dishes, jewelry. When people moved to a new camp every few weeks, they could only own what they could carry. But now they could own as much as their houses could hold.

# Wealth and Power

Owning things can cause problems. People, through hard work and good luck, can come to own more than their neighbors do. And when you have more, you have the power to get even more. With wealth comes greater power—the power to make others do what you want. As people turned to farming, it became possible for a few people to rule over many—to become chiefs, barons and dukes, kings and queens. People had always lived in groups and followed one or more leaders. But now the leaders became different from the people they led. They gathered riches and power to themselves. And even more trouble began.

Another problem with owning things is that somebody else can take them away. Hominids had been facing this trouble from the beginning. They fought to keep their food safe from animals and from other hominids. Fighting between groups has probably occurred for millions of years.

But now people did something that no other creature on Earth had ever done. They fought wars. Led by their rich, powerful kings, people marched out in great armies to conquer other people and steal what they owned. Small villages became mighty cities as the kings grew in wealth and power.

## How Do You Fit In?

But over thousands of years, that wealth and power, born of war, created far greater and more lasting things. Dukes and princes paid for art and poetry and music. Beautiful churches and huge cathedrals rose to the sky. The wealth of kings sent ships to trade with and explore distant lands.

Slowly, wealth spread to more and more people. The rule of law replaced the will of kings. And science replaced the myths by which people lived.

All of this—farming and war, art and law and science—have passed to you from your ancestors. They are gifts from the past, like your skillful hands, your two legs, and your incredible brain. It is up to you to do something with these gifts. Like every human being, you have the power to decide how you want to live and what you want to be. And that may be the most precious gift of all.

59

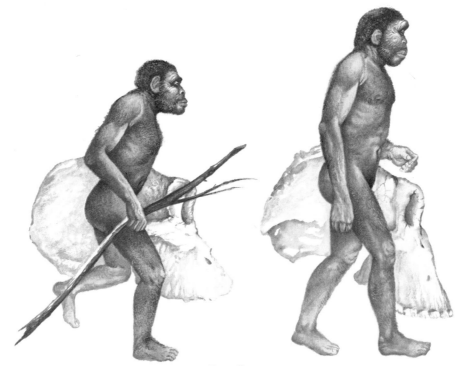

# Index

## A

Adaptation, 19, 20-21
Africa, 13-15, 23, 26, 30
Animals, taming, 46-47
Apes, 13, 16
Arts, 44-46, 52, 59
Australopithecines, 24-26
    diet, 26
    extinction, 26
    *Homo habilis* and, 24-26
    time dating, 38

## B

Baboons, 26
Bering Strait, 49
Bison, 49, 52
Brain:
    australopithecine, 24-25
    *Homo erectus*, 33
    *Homo habilis*, 16, 21
Burial, Neanderthal, 41

## C

Caves:
    as home, 43
    burial in, 41
    paintings in, 44-46, 52

China, 56
Cities, 58
Climate, 12, 31, 43, 52
Clothing:
    *Homo erectus*, 34
    Neanderthals, 43

## D

Dinosaurs, 8-10, 11

## E

Euphrates River, 54, 56

## F

Farming, 54-57
Fighting, 58-59
Fire, *Homo erectus's* use of, 34
Food:
    australopithecine, 26
    farming, 54-57
    fishing, 51
    *Homo habilis*, 15, 26
    hunting, 33, 43, 46
    taming animals, 46-47

## G

Glaciers, 43, 49, 52
Graves, Shanidar cave, 41

## H

Hands:
    *australopithecine*, 24-25
    *Homo habilis*, 16, 19, 20-21
*Homo erectus*:
    as traveler, 34-35, 48
    brain of, 33
    clothing, 34
    communication, 33
    fire used by, 34
    *Homo habilis*, evolving into, 31, 36-37
    hunting, 33, 34-35
    Neanderthals and, 38-43
    time dating of, 38
*Homo habilis*, 14-27
    adaptation, 19, 20-21
    australopithecines and, 24-26
    brain, 16-19, 21
    diet, 14-15, 26
    evolving into, 36-37
    extinction, 31, 36-37
    food gathering, 20-21
    hands, 16, 20-21
    lifestyle, 14-15

*Homo habilis* (continued)
    sharing, 22-23
    spread of, 23-25
    time dating, 38-39
    toolmaking and use,
        20-21, 28-29
    use of weapons by, 21
    walking on two legs, 16
Hominids, 14-16, 24, 48, 56,
    58
    australopithecines, 24-27
    *Homo sapiens sapiens*,
        45-58
    Neanderthals, 38-45, 48
*Homo sapiens sapiens*,
    45-58
    end of Ice Age, 52-53
    farming, 54-57
    spread of, 48-51
Hunting, 33, 43, 46

**I**

Ice Age, 43, 45, 48-49,
    51
Instinct, 19
Islands, 50-51

**L**

La Marche, France, cave
    painting, 46
Language, *Homo erectus's* use
    of, 33
Lions, 13, 15

**M**

Mammals, 8, 10-13
Monkeys, 13, 16, 26

**N**

Neanderthals, 38-43, 45
    appearance of, 40
    burial by, 40-41
    *Homo erectus* and, 41
    spread of, 42-43
    use of tools by, 41
New Zealand, 50

**P**

Pacific Oceans islands, 50
Population growth, 54
Power, 58-59

**R**

Reindeer, 49, 52

**S**

Seeds, planting, 55, 56
Shanidar cave, 41
Sharing by *Homo habilis*,
    22-23
South America, farming in,
    56
Stone tools, 28-29, 33, 41
Study of primitive man, 28-29

**T**

Tigris River, 54, 56
Tools:
    *Homo habilis's* use, 21
    measuring age, 38
    Neanderthal, 41
    stone, 28-29, 33, 41
Towns, growth, 57

**V**

Villages, growth of, 57
Volcanoes, 10

**W**

Walking on two legs, 16, 24
War, 58-59
Warm-blooded animals, 8
Woolly mammoth, 13

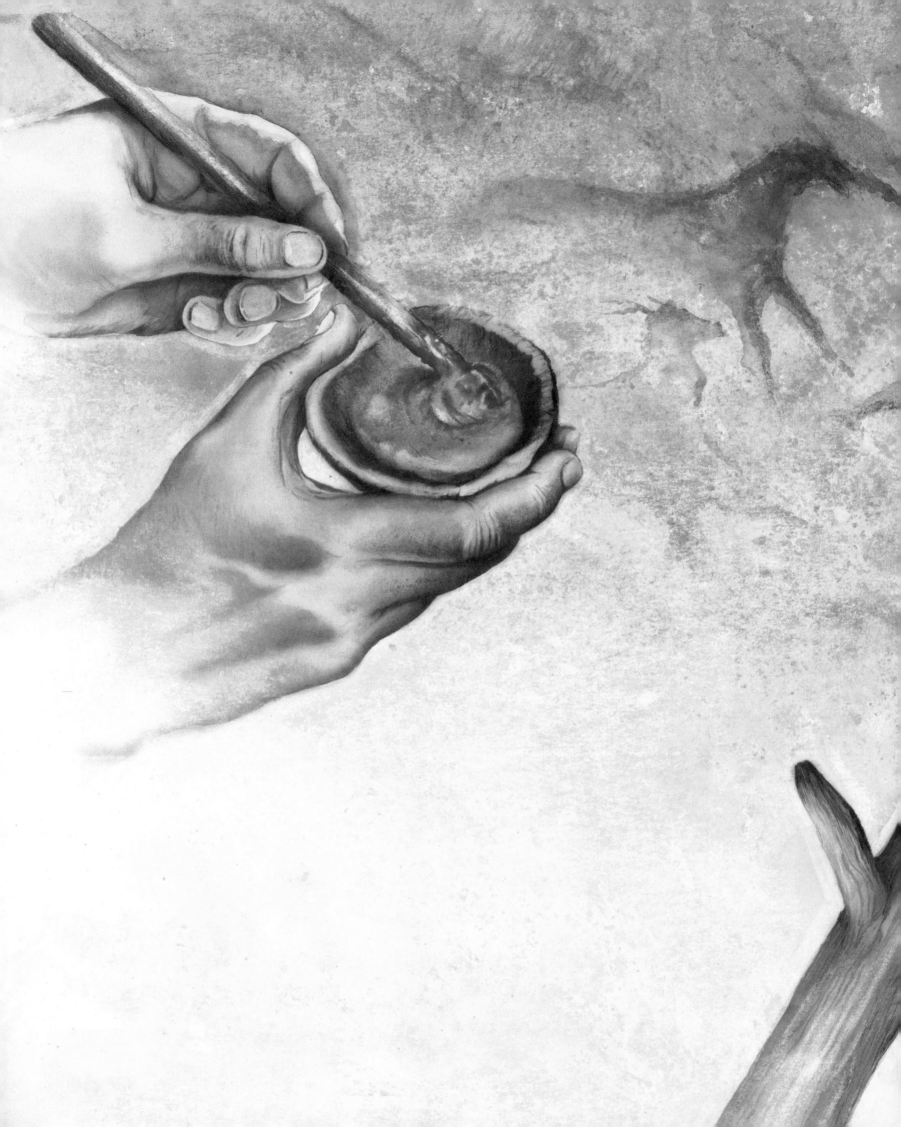